Bear on the Homefront

Stephanie Innes &
Harry Endrulat

ART BY Brian Deines

pajamapress

First published in the United States in 2014

Text copyright © 2014 Stephanie Innes and Harry Endrulat
Illustration copyright © 2014 Brian Deines
This edition copyright © 2014 Pajama Press Inc.
This is a first edition.

10 9 8 7 6 5 4 3 2 1

www.pajamapress.ca   info@pajamapress.ca

 Canada Council   Conseil des Arts
for the Arts   du Canada    ONTARIO ARTS COUNCIL
CONSEIL DES ARTS DE L'ONTARIO

The publisher gratefully acknowledges the support of the Canada Council for the Arts and the Ontario Arts Council for its publishing program. We acknowledge the financial support of the Government of Canada through the Canada Book Fund for our publishing activities.

Library and Archives Canada Cataloguing in Publication

Innes, Stephanie, author   Bear on the homefront / Stephanie Innes, Harry Endrulat ; Brian Deines, illustrator.

ISBN 978-1-927485-13-2 (bound)

    1. World War, 1939-1945--Children--Great Britain--Juvenile literature.   2. World War, 1939-1945--Children--Canada--Juvenile literature. 3. Teddy bears--Juvenile literature. I. Endrulat, Harry, author II. Deines, Brian, illustrator III. Title.

DC810.C4I55 2014   j940.53>161   C2013-907317-5

Publisher Cataloging-in-Publication Data (U.S.)

Endrulat, Harry, 1964-

    Bear on the homefront / Harry Endrulat ; Stephanie Innes ; Brian Deines.

[32] pages : col. ill. ; cm.

Summary: During World War II, nurse Aileen Rogers and her stuffed bear, Teddy, greet English "guest children" sent overseas for safety. Teddy befriends homesick, young William and his sister Grace, sharing the experience of the cross-country train ride and five years on a host family's farm.

ISBN-13: 978-1-927485-13-2

1. World War, 1939-1945 – Children – Great Britain – Juvenile literature. 2. World War, 1939-1945 – Children — Canada – Juvenile literature. 3. Teddy bears – Juvenile literature. I. Innes, Stephanie, 1965- II. Deines, Brian, 1955- , ill. III. Title.

940.53/161 dc23   DC810.C4E64 2014

Cover and book design by Martin Gould
Children's hand-writing by Arielle Deines
Original art created with oil paints on canvas

Manufactured by Sheck Wah Tong Printing Ltd.
Printed in Hong Kong, China

Pajama Press Inc.
181 Carlaw Ave., Suite 207,
Toronto, Ontario Canada, M4M 2S1

Distributed in Canada by UTP Distribution
5201 Dufferin Street Toronto, Ontario Canada, M3H 5T8

Distributed in the U.S. by Orca Book Publishers
PO Box 468 Custer, WA, 98240-0468, USA

For Hannah, Duncan, Hilary, Sebastian, Dominic, Haley, and Nick.
  –S.I.

For Mom, Dad, and Shirley – for your continued love and support.
And for Cathy, Hayley, and Harrison – my inspiration.
  –H.E.

For Arielle and Lisa.
Sébastien, you are a champion!
  –B.D.

The August air was warm and the sky was blue on the day the guest children came to Canada. The big ship that had carried them across the ocean landed in Halifax Harbour, Nova Scotia.

I watched from the pocket of Aileen's uniform as the children walked down the ramp.

"Where are their mummies and daddies?" I asked.

"Still overseas," Aileen said. "England is being bombed in the war, so many families have sent their children to Canada, where they'll be safe."

A band started to play on the dock and some of the children sang along.

"There'll always be an England, and England shall be free.
If England means as much to you as England means to me."

But two of the smallest children weren't singing. They looked lost and afraid. Aileen went over and introduced herself.

"My name is Grace," replied the young girl in a soft voice. "And this is my brother, William. He is five."

Grace pointed to me. "Who's that?"

"This is Teddy," Aileen said.

William peeked his head out from behind his sister.

Aileen and the other nurses helped the children with their suitcases and matched their names to a list.

"The children will be going to families all over Canada," Aileen explained. "It's our job to make sure they arrive safely."

We took the children to the train station. Many ran and played games, happy to be off the boat, but William and Grace didn't join in.

Grace looked at her younger brother and frowned. "He wants to go home," she told Aileen. "Everything here seems so strange."

"When the war is over, everyone will go home," Aileen said. "Until then, we'll do our best to make sure you are safe and sound."

"And I can keep you company," I said.

Aileen held me out to William. He stared at me for a long time. Then he took me carefully into his arms.

It was late when we finally boarded the train. Aileen showed the children how the seats turned into beds, and Grace and William lay down side by side. I was tired too.

"There's room for you, Teddy," Grace said. I snuggled between them.

"Good night, William," I whispered.

William looked down at me for a moment. At last he smiled. "Good night, Teddy."

The next morning, William held me up to the window.

Grace said, "Aileen told me we are going to live on a farm in Winnipeg."

"I'm scared of strangers," said William. "What if they are horrid and smell and won't give us anything to eat?"

Grace smiled bravely. "They want to keep us safe until the war is over. I think they will be kind."

"Just like Aileen," I said.

Aileen was busy. When we were in Saint John, New Brunswick, she helped a boy who'd gotten a cinder in his eye when he stuck his head out the window. The cinder came from the train's firebox.

At our stop in Montreal, the Red Cross brought plates of biscuits and hot milk. Some of the children ate too much and became sick. Aileen gave them medicine for their tummies and stayed with them until they felt better.

One morning, Aileen sat with us in the dining car. While we waited for our porridge, Aileen wrote in her diary and Grace told me a secret.

"Mummy gave me a letter she wrote to the Winnipeg family," she said. "Would you like to see it?"

I nodded.

To whom it may concern:

My husband Charles and I are grateful that you will care for Grace and William until the war is finished. We pray that it will be soon.

Please tell them their mummy and daddy love them.

With deepest thanks,
Lizzie Chambers

When the train stopped in North Bay, Ontario, people met us on the platform with fruit and toys for the children. One man even played the bagpipes!

Some of the children got off to meet their families.

One boy received a large truck and wouldn't let it out of his hands. Another was given a book.

William accepted a ball, and Grace's present was a soft blue bag filled with marbles. We each picked out our favorites. Mine was yellow, Grace's was red, and William's was clear. Grace told us we could make a wish on our marbles.

"I wish the Winnipeg family will be kind," she said.

"I wish that the war will end soon," William said.

"I wish that too," I said.

By the next evening, we were close to Winnipeg. The children were excited to see the city lights. Some threw off their covers and tossed pillows around. Others hung from the beds like monkeys! Grace and William sat quietly holding hands.

It was almost midnight when we reached the railway station.

Aileen put me in her pocket. We stepped off the train and stood on the platform in the dark.

"Grace and William?" said a smiling woman.

Grace nodded.

"I am Mrs. Dent and this is my husband. You are coming to live with us on our farm."

Grace stepped forward and shook hands with Mr. and Mrs. Dent, but William stayed next to Aileen. "I don't want to go," he said quietly. "I want to stay with you."

I looked at Aileen and nodded.

Aileen picked me up and hugged me. Then she handed me to William.

"I'll stay with you," I said.

William held me tight.

"All aboard!" the conductor yelled.

"Take good care of the children," Aileen said as she patted my head. I knew I was going to miss her, but she had more children to help. Aileen waved as the train pulled away from the station.

"You look sad, Teddy," said William.

"I wonder if I will ever see Aileen again."

William nodded. "That's how I felt when I left my parents in England."

Mr. and Mrs. Dent helped us into their truck and we drove away. By the time we arrived at their old stone farmhouse, the children were fast asleep.

Mrs. Dent carried William upstairs. Mr. Dent carried Grace.

"Should we wake them and help them into their nightclothes?" whispered Mr. Dent.

Mrs. Dent shook her head. "Let them be. They've had a long journey."

She placed a blue quilt over William and a red one over Grace.

The next morning, we tiptoed downstairs and peeked into the kitchen. Mrs. Dent was by the stove, flipping eggs in a cast-iron pan.

Mr. Dent poured coffee into his mug.

"In London we drink tea," Grace said.

"Then I will make you a cup," Mrs. Dent said with a smile.

After breakfast Mr. Dent took us outside and pointed to the fields in the distance.

"We used to grow only wheat, but prices are low. Now we grow other crops like oats and rye."

Next, he took us to the barn. We saw cows, horses, chickens, a dog, and some cats.

"On a farm, everyone pitches in," Mr. Dent said. "We feed the chickens, gather the eggs, milk the cows, and help in the fields. Do you think you can do that?"

Grace nodded, but William looked worried.

"I'll help you," I whispered.

William nodded too.

"Good lad," said Mr. Dent.

By the time fall arrived, we had become used to our new routine.

In the morning we got up before the sun. William collected eggs from the chickens and Grace helped Mr. Dent milk the cow.

After breakfast we went to school. We learned that lots of Canadians were in Europe fighting with the British.

"I'm scared for Mum and Dad," Grace said.

"Me too," William said.

In December, it started to snow.

The children hoped Santa would find them in Canada.

They wrote a letter to their parents:

Dear Mum and Dad,

We've been getting ready for Christmas. Mr. Dent took us into the bush and cut down a giant pine. It was almost too big to get through the door! We decorated the tree with paper snowflakes and white candles.

We miss you and pray that the war will end soon so we can be together again.

Love,
William and Grace

That night after Mr. and Mrs. Dent tucked us into bed, William asked me a question.

"Do you miss Aileen?" he said.

I nodded.

"I miss my mum and dad a lot," he said. "I don't like the war. I hope it ends soon."

"Me too," I said.

But the war did not end soon. It went on for five years, until William's tenth birthday.

Then it was time for William and Grace to go home.

One morning, not long after William and Grace left
Canada, a package was delivered to the Montreal hospital
where Aileen worked.

Inside was a soft blue bag
and a letter.

> Dearest Aileen,
> Thank you for allowing Teddy
> to stay with us during the war.
> We would have been terribly
> lonely without him.
>
> Since we are going home now,
> Teddy needs to go home too.
>
> Love,
> William and Grace

"Teddy!" Aileen cried as she opened the bag.

I was sad to say good-bye to William and Grace, but I
was very happy to see Aileen.

Finally, we were all back home, where we belonged.

Like Teddy's first story, *A Bear in War*, *Bear on the Homefront* is inspired by a family's experience during war. The book is based on a diary that Aileen Rogers kept in 1940, when she was a nurse helping deliver guest children from war-torn England to host families across Canada.

About 15,000 children were evacuated overseas from London both privately and through a government program. Canada received about 1,300 of the children that came through the short-lived Children's Overseas Reception Board, which the British government created in May 1940. The government program ended just four months later when a ship carrying ninety child evacuees was hit by a German torpedo. Seventy-seven of the children died.

Teddy, the tiny stuffed bear in both *Bear* books, was given to Aileen in the early 1900s when she was a young girl living on a farm in East Farnham, Quebec.

Aileen sent her beloved Teddy to her father, Lieutenant Lawrence Browning Rogers, when he was fighting on the front lines during World War I. Lawrence died at the Battle of Passchendaele on October 30, 1917.

In 2002, Lawrence's granddaughter, Roberta Rogers Innes, found Teddy and other war memorabilia in a large family briefcase. The items inside included more than 200 letters that had been exchanged between Lawrence and his family during World War I. *A Bear in War* is based on those letters.

Teddy now sits in the Canadian War Museum in Ottawa, Ontario.

Aileen's travel diary